The Crocodile
& The Hippo

The Crocodile & The Hippo

Hubert Severe

XULON PRESS

Xulon Press
2301 Lucien Way #415
Maitland, FL 32751
407.339.4217
www.xulonpress.com

Unless otherwise indicated, Scripture quotations taken from the International Children's Bible (ICB). The Holy Bible, International Children's Bible® Copyright© 1986, 1988, 1999, 2015 by Tommy Nelson™, a division of Thomas Nelson. Used by permission.

Paperback ISBN-13: 978-1-66285-901-4
Ebook ISBN-13: 978-1-66285-902-1

Welcome Parents
And Children

This is a story my grandmother's father used to tell her. My grandmother shared it with me when I was old enough to understand the truth. It taught me how and why I should treat others better than myself even though they are my worst enemies. Parents and children, I want to introduce this story to you by sharing this powerful truth with you.

The Best Way To Do Things Is The Right Way.

Sometimes we make mistakes, but if that happens, we still need to try to correct them if at all possible. When we are baking something, we use a good recipe to make good food. When we follow the good recipe and do what it says, we end up with good food. Doing things that are right in our lives also brings a good life and we will find that doing things the right way is also the easy way.

My grandmother used to tell me, "When you do things for others, you should never expect things in return. When we do good things for others, we should never regret what we did because the Lord watches and remembers everything we do. When our life starts getting harder, it is because our blessing is getting closer, and we don't want to miss it. This is one of the reasons we should do things the right way and wait for our blessing to come. Always remember, our blessings come from the Lord."

We must not become tired of doing good. We will receive our harvest of eternal life at the right time. We must not give up! (Galatians 6:9 ICB)[1]

---

[1] Taken from the International Children's Bible (ICB) The Holy Bible, International Children's Bible® Copyright© 1986, 1988, 1999, 2015 by Tommy Nelson™, a division of Thomas Nelson. Used by permission.

Meet The Crocodile
And The Hippo

The crocodiles and the hippos were living together in the same neighborhood. They were the best neighbors anyone could have ever wanted. They helped each other in all different matters, even though they did not look the same or eat the same foods.

They used to say, "Anyone who truly believes in God should never look at one another by color, race, or religion. We are all the children of God, and it doesn't matter how we look."

The hippo family was not as large as the crocodile family. However, they weren't afraid of each other, and they lived peacefully together just like one big family.

One hippo named Andrew and his wife Miranda were very happy even though they didn't have much. They always said the best way to really be happy in life is by helping and blessing others as the Lord had blessed them. They knew how to following the rules of life the right way and working to make life easy for everyone else brings them true happiness. They also knew when we do or say things to hurt others, in the long run, we are the ones who are hurt the most.

Life isn't about color, race, or religion, it is about how we work together to receive the blessing of God together. We all deserve happiness, and we should do our best to do things to make each other happy no matter what happens in our lives.

Parents, pause for a moment and ask your child(ren) these simple questions to encourage them to understand the truths presented so far.

Ask your child to answer these True or False questions:

The hippos live in the same area as the crocodiles.

The hippo family was bigger than the crocodile family.

The hippo family and the crocodile family were different.

Ask your child how the crocodiles and the hippos were different from each other.

Ask if they remember the names of the hippos in our story.

Fill in the blanks:

How we treat others isn't about their _____,
_____, or _____.

Use age-appropriate terminology to discuss the terms "color, race, and religion" as this concept pertains to the story so far.

Meet Yalda And Zhi

Andrew and Miranda had a very cute little baby girl they named Yalda. They were very happy and loved their baby. The crocodile families were happy for them. When they come to see Yalda, they brought something for her and showed her love. The crocodile family's children played with her more than the hippo family.

There was a big crocodile named Zhi. He was the oldest croc of them all. Everyone in both groups loved to take advice from him. All the families wished for their kids to be just like him.

Zhi was quiet, wise, and lovingly taught the children the important concepts of life.

- "You have one life and a million lives around you. When you take care of the million lives around you, you automatically take care of your life. You always need to have your hand ready to offer help to another."

- Remember: "We must not become tired of doing good. We will receive our harvest of eternal life at the right time. We must not give up!"[2] (Galatians 6:9 ICB)

- "We make mistakes, however, the Lord didn't. The reason things are bad in our lives is because we do things wrong and use things the wrong way. It is not the Lord's fault."

- "We all know the truth of how God wants us to do things so we should not let anyone come into our lives and destroy all the good things we have been working so hard for by trying to show us an easy way out. The Lord's way is the right way."

- "We can try to fool others, but we can never fool the Lord. The day we realize that truth is the day our world will become better."

---

[2] Galatians 6:9 ICB International Children's Bible (ICB) The Holy Bible, International Children's Bible® Copyright© 1986, 1988, 1999, 2015 by Tommy Nelson™, a division of Thomas Nelson. Used by permission.

Parents, pause for a moment and ask your child(ren) these simple questions to encourage them to understand the truths presented so far.

What is the baby hippo's name?

How many lives did we learn each of us has?

What can happen when you help take care of your neighbors?

Is it good to take advantage of others?

    Why or why not?

If we take care of our world in God's way, what will happen?

Why are things sometimes bad in our lives?

In your own words, what do we need to do to make the world a better place to live?

Explain what it means to not get tired of doing good.

When Yalda was a few weeks old, her mother left her with her father and never returned. Yalda stayed with her father and the other hippo families. She was so young she did not understand all that was happening in her life. All the families in the community helped to take care of her. Everyone who had babies helped feed her, even the crocodiles. She was one of the happiest kids in the town. Her father was her best friend. He always taught her the truth even though sometimes she was too young to understand his point.

One day, her father said to her, "I have already received my blessing from the Lord and my family. Now, it's up to me to do things right to keep this blessing continuing in my life. It's time for me to show I can be the best father by doing things a father should do for his child. I love you so much my little Yalda and unless I die, I will not let anything happen to you. I want to show you how to do the things you need to do to live life the right way. You just need to listen to me and the other people who want to help you to do things right. Follow us the right way and obey the rules and then you will see how good your life can be."

Parents, pause for a moment and ask your child(ren) these simple questions to encourage them to understand the truths presented so far.

Who was the little hippo left to live with?

Why?

What do you think may have happened to Yalda's mother?

Why was Yalda one of the happiest kids in the town?

Are you one of the happiest kids in your town?

> *Why or why not?*

Should a parent let bad things happen to their kids?

Do you think your parents love you?

> *Why or why not?*

In your own words, what do you need to do to show your parents you appreciate all the things they have done for you?

In your own words, what do you need to do to make you and your parents happy?

In your own words, why do you think some kids don't like to listen to their parents?

Month after month the baby hippo grew. Her best friend became Mr. Zhi. Mr. Zhi was very nice to all the children. He said all the kids in the community should get the same love whether they are yours or not. He was connected with Yalda and Yalda was connected to him, too. One day, the little hippo asked him a question.

She said, "I can see you eat anything that moves, and I can see we are different from each other. Why do you and your families protect us and never do anything bad to us hippos?"

The crocodile said, "Listen, my little girl. Your eyes are the ones who see us differently, but deep inside of us we are the same. Why do you think we live together, love each other, and help one another in all our needs? My little girl, a good and smart neighbor doesn't take things from his neighbors or his race or his nation. They work together and have each other's backs all the time. This is called being united. Good neighbors should protect each other and be not afraid of one another."

Mr. Zhi smiled at his young student and said, "My little girl, life doesn't just come our way anyway it wants, but the way we want. Neighbors need to understand that God our Father does not want us hurting each other for things He has given us to share with one another. We need to understand we will leave them behind when we are gone for those who come after us. That is the way God designed our lives to work."

Pointing to the crocodiles and hippos all around them, Mr. Zhi told her, "We are the ones who should bring peace to our communities. Our Father God gave us life and tools like the special things we know how to do to make a great life for ourselves and for our communities. It is time for us to work together to use these tools to bring freedom, peace, joy, happiness, and all the things that could make us have a happy life. Each of us needs to do our part."

Parents, pause for a moment and ask your child(ren) these simple questions to encourage them to understand the truths presented so far.

True or False:

Yalda's best friend was a hippo named Mr. Zhi.

Everyone should be nice to kids.

Bringing Peace to Our Community:

Why should we be nice to each other?

What do we need to do to protect each other?

Do you believe that we are the same?

Do you believe that we should connect with each other?

What can we each do to bring peace to our lives?

Do you believe we should share with each other?

What special tools (talents) did our Father God give you?

Do you know how to use the tools our Father God gave you?

Are you going to show others how to use their special tools (talents)?

Do you have peace, joy, and happiness in your life?

Explain why you do or do not:

The little hippo was getting smarter and understanding things better. Since she was so close to him, she called Zhi, Uncle Croc. She loved to ask him questions and believed he would give her the right answer.

One day, she said, "Uncle Croc, I want to ask you a question."

Uncle Croc said, "What is it, my little girl?"

"Why do humans kill each other and drop them here in our community?" she asked him.

He answered, "Listen, my little girl, humans should be one of the smartest creatures on earth, but they are not. When you look at the things human beings are doing, you will judge them as the dumbest creatures on earth. The Lord gives human beings the power to control the world. They should be using that power to make the world a better place for all God's creatures, but they are destroying the world because of selfishness. Humans do everything the opposite way they should, but by the time they see the truth, it will probably be too late. We need to get ready because a day is coming when our Heavenly Father will grow tired of their nonsense. He will take their power and give it to us. I know we will do a better job than the humans have been doing. Hesaid, humans can train us animal's to be the best pals and it doesn't matter how we hated each others and they can't train themselves to be friends and hesaid, I can't understand why."

Surprised, Yalda looked at Uncle Croc wondering what he meant by this.

Seeing the confusion in her eyes, Uncle Croc continued, "After all the time humans have had this power, I don't see anything good they do with it. I have lived many, many years and have seen how when humans come into an area, peace, joy, happiness, and all other things we have for a good life are destroyed. Human beings think anything that doesn't look like them is a problem, and they will do anything to destroy it, including themselves. Human beings seem unable to understand these truths I have been teaching you. The best way for us to have a good life is to stay away from them."

Parents, pause for a moment and ask your child(ren) these simple questions to encourage them to understand the truths presented so far.

Do you believe human beings are the smartest creatures on earth?

Do you believe we are doing good things to save our planet?

Who has our Father God given the power to control the world?

Are they using the power the right way?

What does it mean to be selfish?

Do you think humans are selfish?

One day, Yalda went out to find good grass with her father and another animal snapped at her. Her father was able to keep her safe and nothing happened to her. When she got home, she ran to Uncle Croc and told him what happened.

He said, "Life is divided into many different types of creatures. This is called the circle of life. There are humans, animals, birds, and fish. We all do different things to keep our family cared for and safe, but we should never do bad things to do it. It's only human beings who don't understand they need to work together to keep their family and community safe. Have you seen how I carefully carry my children in my mouth, and I never mistake and bite them?"

Uncle Croc smiled at her and said, "Everything we do should be to care for each other. However, selfishness can make a creature become the worst evil thing on earth. That creature that snapped at you probably wanted the grass where you were eating. Every bad thing that has happened on this planet came out of selfishness. If allowed to become part of your life, selfishness encourages you to only see yourself. The Lord says you need to always try to see the needs of others first.[3] Even though you don't have much, as long as you have love in your life, you can look at yourself as the richest animal on earth."

Seeing some confusion in her expression, Uncle Croc explained, "Listen, my little girl, your eyes and your mind can cause you to look at and want things if you don't use them right. That becomes selfishness and is why you see others destroy one another for things they want. They don't realize they have more than the one they destroyed. My little girl, there is something our Father God has given each of us called common sense, however, some never use it. Please, use yours and you will see how full your life can be."

Parents, pause for a moment and ask your child(ren) these simple questions to encourage them to understand the truths presented so far.

What is selfishness?

---

[3] Read Philippians 2:3, "When you do things, do not let selfishness or pride be your guide. Be humble and give more honor to others than to yourselves" (ICB).

What does selfishness encourage you to do?

What is the best thing you need in life?

Do you know what common sense is?

Do you use yours or know how to use it?

Do you judge yourself as a good or a bad person?

Why?

One day, Yalda asked Uncle Croc, "I don't understand. Some say we shouldn't talk to strangers and others say we have to be nice to everyone. I am confused. Which is right?"

Uncle Croc said, "Let me explain it to you the right way so you will not be confused. Right now, we are living in a world where others don't try to help. In fact, they hurt others who are different or over things they want. We should use our command sense to do things carefully and the right way. We need to respect, appreciate, help, and love everyone who wants our help no matter their color, race, or religion. Please, don't be like human beings who hurt those who are not like them."

Uncle Croc then warned her, "However, you shouldn't be too friendly to others you don't know, especially when you are by yourself. You shouldn't give strangers any of your personal information, follow them, or go places with them. If you want to go somewhere with someone, your father needs to know all about him or her. Listen, safety is the key of your life, and you need this key with you all the time. Don't do the foolish things you might see human beings doing to one another. Human beings are the worst living creatures, and you should never want to take advice from them or do what they tell you to do. Do you understand?"

Parents, pause for a moment and ask your child(ren) these simple questions to encourage them to understand the truths presented so far.

Do you believe we should be nice and help each other?

Why should kids not be friendly or talk to strangers?

List the things you shouldn't do with or tell strangers:

Do you think if we respect, appreciate, support, love, help, and work together, we will have a better life?

Do you believe we should choose who we want to help or help everyone who needs our help?

One day, the little hippo was having an interesting conversation with Uncle Croc about safety.

He said, "Life in our community with our families and friends should be the best times in our lives. However, anywhere we live where human beings are around, our lives will not be safe or easy. I don't really understand why."

Uncle Croc shook his head sadly, "Look at us, we don't need weapons to be secure our lives. Human beings created a lot of weapons and things to destroy one another. Listen, my little girl, how can they say they have a good country when they take all the guns from the police and give them to the citizens to protect themselves. Soon humans will be worst than the wild dogs and hyenas that kill each other and don't even know why. We know the best way to make peace in a community is to make everyone follow the laws. The leaders should be the ones who model respect and follow the law first."

"As a leader in this community, I want you to understand, my little girl, that I love you more than if you were one of my family," Uncle Croc told her. "When I am gone, I want you to be the one who takes my spot. I can see you as the only one who deserves it. If you ever have the power to communicate with human beings, please explain to them all the mistakes they have made in their lives and how far they could be ahead if they would choose to do things right. Please let them know the meaning of being like brothers and sisters and how to praise the Lord for all their blessings. As those who believe in God, they should follow the Lord's rules, and commands, and use their common sense to do things right. We should never hate, take advantage of, or fight each other for anything unless it is to save a life."

Parents, pause for a moment and ask your child(ren) these simple questions to encourage them to understand the truths presented so far.

> *Do you believe we are secure in our homes, our communities, our schools, and our cities?*

> *Do you respect the rules of God and the laws?*

> *What do you do to show those around you that you are doing your part the right way to make our world safer and a better place to live?*

> *What makes you believe you are a Christian?*

One day, the little hippo asked Uncle Croc, "You are always talking to me about love, but how can I grow love inside of me?"

Uncle Croc answered, "Growing love inside of you is the easiest thing in life. I don't understand why others make it so difficult. The best way is to share your love with others even if you have never received love from them. For example, if you are traveling in any type of transportation and see an elderly, pregnant, or disabled animal, what should you do?"

She answered, "I will get up and give them my seat."

"That is correct," Uncle Croc told her with a smile. "Unfortunately, human beings don't even know love grows inside of you when you do nice things for others. Love will grow inside the other person you help, too. This is one of the reasons heaven and hell have one entrance. You just need to do your best to get to heaven's entrance. Please, don't let things you see make you enter the wrong entrance because of laziness, jealousy, or hatred. The Lord is patient with His children and wants to see them enter into the right entrance and join Him in heaven by doing things the right way."

Parents, pause for a moment and ask your child(ren) these simple questions to encourage them to understand the truths presented so far.

Do you know what love means?

List a few things that can cause love to grow in your life:

Do you love to share?

Do you believe we all should know when to do good things for each other?

If you know how many people you have helped, that means you haven't helped enough. Do you know how many people you have helped?

Do you know how to get to the entrance of heaven?

Are you a lazy or hard-working kid?

What do you do when you see someone who really needs your seat when you are traveling?

Do you understand right and wrong, and good and bad?

Do your parents have patience with you?

Do you respect, love, and appreciate your parents?

One day, Yalda said to Uncle Croc, "I watch my dad and I can see he has a lot of problems. I wish I could help him."

Uncle Croc said, "Your dad doesn't need help. I have offered him my assistance. He has learned there are some problems no one can help with unless he begins to help himself. He is doing that right now. Stress is a big problem in many lives. Stress is not like a headache. There have been many famous animals who died because of stress. Please, my little girl, don't you ever let that happen to you. You need to always be on top of your problems. When a problem comes, you need to find the best way to get rid of it immediately before it damages something in you. Sometimes, we believe problems are easy things to handle, but if you find you need help, please ask for it."

"The worst kind are family problems. Any family member who wants to bring you nothing but problems you need to stay away from them. I want you to understand that smoking, drinking alcohol, or taking any type of drugs will not help you with your problems. These things will make it worse. The best way to overcome your problems is to fight them and if you need help please let others know. You need to be very careful because some animals will make your problems worse. Do you understand?"

Yalda said, "Yes."

Parents, pause for a moment and ask your child(ren) these simple questions to encourage them to understand the truths presented so far.

When your parents have problems, do they solve the problems without you being involved with them?

Do you know what problems can do to you?

Do you know how to solve your problems?

Do you double-check with your parents to make sure you overcome them the right way?

What do you about people who bring you nothing but problems?

Do you think smoking, drinking alcohol, or taking drugs will help you with your problems?

What will they do with your problems?

Who do you really trust to help you overcome your problems?

What is the best way to get rid of your problems?

A Sunday afternoon after Yalda came from church with her father, she was having a loud conversation with her father about cleaning. Mr. Zhi passed by and heard them talking.

The next day, he asked Yalda, "What happened with you and your dad yesterday?"

She said, "My dad kept complaining about how I only help him clean sometimes."

Mr. Zhi asked her, "Do you sometimes eat, drink, or put on clean clothes?"

"No," she answered. "I do those every single day."

Mr. Zhi said, "So you need to clean yourself and your living area every single day, too. Listen, my girl, you need to listen to your father more than you listen to me. Your family has a true love for you and always wants the best for you. Please, my little girl, maybe you don't listen when I talk to you. If you do, then you need to start doing things right. Cleaning is something we need to do all the time, not just when we want to. Now, young kids don't understand they need to keep themselves clean all the time. You are old enough to know that you need to bathe, brush your teeth, clean your nails and toenails, and your living area daily. This helps you to have better health. Remember, a cute little girl means a clean little girl."

Parents, pause for a moment and ask your child(ren) these simple questions to encourage them to understand the truths presented so far.

Do you sometimes have loud conversations with your parents?

What are a few things your parents ask you to help them with?

Do you listen to your parents and do what they ask?

Are you a clean kid?

Do you always shower, brush your teeth, fix your bed when you wake up, and do things a clean person does every day?

What do you think may happen if you do not do these things daily?

Why is it important to keep yourself and where you live clean?

One day, the little hippo asked Uncle Croc, "Why are parents nicer to other kids than theirs?"

Uncle Croc said, "Do you remember when I gave you the piece of bread yesterday and you said it tasted good? That came from what your father baked for you. He gave some to you and you said that it was yak, yet when I gave it to you, you said it was yummy. How many times are you nicer to me than to your father? You do anything I ask you to, but when your father asks you to do something, he is lucky if you do it. When you wake up, do you tell your dad good morning, yet don't you always wish me good morning?"

The little hippo began to understand what Uncle Croc was saying, "The truth is, my little girl, your father may seem nicer to other kids than to you, but he will never love any other kid better than you. Your father has a special love for you, even if he does not always say it to you. We are supposed to love each other, but our first love should be for our family. Do you understand me, little one?"

"Yes, Uncle Croc," she said with a smile. "You mean my first love should be for my dad. I need to show my family how much I love them without them having to guess. I love you, too, Uncle Croc."

Uncle Croc said, "I love you, too, little girl."

Then Yalda went to her father and gave him a big hug without saying why.

Parents, pause for a moment and ask your child(ren) these simple questions to encourage them to understand the truths presented so far.

When you wake up, do you tell your parents good morning?

Are you nice to your parents the same way you want them to be nice to you?

When was the last time you did something nice for your parents?

Do you believe your parents love someone better than you?

Who?

Who do you give the first love in your heart to?

Does he or she deserve it?

One day, the little hippo asked Uncle Croc, "Your grandson Llya said Satan blesses us quicker than the Lord. Is that true?"

Uncle Croc said, "I would love to answer your question, but I do not think you are ready for the answer yet."

She said, "I'm ready. Please answer me, Uncle Croc."

He said, "If you think you are ready, tell me what happens when you run the race with the other kids, and you do not come in first?"

She said, "I congratulate the winner and am determined to work harder the next time."

He said, "You are correct. I see that you are ready to hear the truth. You know I love you so much and you are my girl. Llya is my grandson and I love him, too. Love is something we grow within us, but sometimes we react to how they treat us. This is the reason we can love and hate each other. The more others hate you or do bad things to you, the more you need to love them. All they are doing is blocking their blessing from God, but we do not have to react the way they do. Do you understand that little one?"

When Yalda nodded she did, Uncle Croc continued, "Listen, my little girl, even though we can't see God and Satan, they are there. When you talk to our Father God in prayer, you need to understand He hears you and He sees your need. However, He will not give you something that will hurt you or others. Satan may seem to answer your wish quickly, but he will never give you what you really need. Satan always wants you to come back to him and beg for more. When the Lord blesses you with the things you need, it is a forever blessing. You need to be very careful with the choices you make. Do not be confused concerning our Father God who gives only good gifts designed to give you a good life, while Satan is a liar, a deceiver, and wants to destroy your life."

Parents, pause for a moment and ask your child(ren) these simple questions to encourage them to understand the truths presented so far.

Do you believe in God?

Do you believe in Satan?

Does Father God give things to get things in return?

When you take things from Satan, what could happen?

Who seems to give things quicker, the Lord or Satan?

Do you understand getting something quicker might bring you pain instead of happiness?

One Saturday morning, Mr. Zhi went to Yalda's home to see her. He had heard she wasn't feeling well, and he went to see what was wrong with her. He brought medicine for her father to make tea for her. He stayed there for a while and shared some good stories with her. Even though she was sick, she was laughing the whole time he was there. After a few days, she got better.

When she was better, Mr. Zhi took her to buy something for her dad and he asked her, "How many friends came to visit you when you were sick?"

"Four," she answered.

He explained, "Those four who came to visit you were your true friends. When you are sick or having problems, you find out who are really your friends."

He said, "Little girl, don't ever use anyone or take advantage of anyone. The Lord doesn't like that. Remember the Lord created us to bless one another. The Lord does not want only a few of us to be happy. He wants all of us to be happy even though we choose the wrong direction sometimes. He wants us to follow the right direction so we will not lose our way. If human beings understood this, they would have a better life than they have right now. They want to blame each other rather than correct each other when they make mistakes. My little girl, this is one of the reasons we struggle sometimes. It is time for us to stand up, admit when we make a mistake, and turn back to the right path before it is too late."

Parents, pause for a moment and ask your child(ren) these simple questions to encourage them to understand the truths presented so far.

What do you do when your best friend is sick?

Who is really your true friend?

Have you ever blamed someone else for your mistakes?

Do you believe in forgiveness?

What do you do when you see someone who is making a mistake?

Do you like to share your thoughts or knowledge with others?

One day, when Mr. Zhi went to Yalda's house, she and her father were working on a project together. Yalda and her father were happy to see him. As they worked together, they started having a conversation about good and bad behavior.

Mr. Zhi said, "It is so good to see you two working together. When kids listen to their parent's instructions, they can do things the right way. However, when kids don't listen to their parents, they make the worst mistakes in their lives. They begin to think they know more than we do because we didn't go to school. They don't understand that when we talk to them about something it is because we already got hurt by it and we don't want them to get hurt the same way. They don't understand we love them more than we love ourselves. I have seen some kids complain about things their parents say they aren't supposed to do, but they don't understand what their parents are doing for them."

Then he turned to Yalda and said, "Listen, my little girl, you don't need to be in a dangerous situation to realize your father is always trying to protect you from getting hurt. You need to try your best to learn from us. Do you see those of us who have a good life and relationships with our families are the ones where the kids listen to their parents? It is important that you listen and do not refuse to do things that are right. You are very smart, and you know the right way is the best way."

After Mr. Zhi left, her father was very happy with the way Mr. Zhi talked to her.

Her father said, "I'm a single parent and even though I don't have too much, I do my best to take great care of you. You know how much I really love you. I don't understand, though, why sometimes you do not trust me when I tell you how to do things the right way. I can't force you to do things that are right, but when the time comes for you to make choices, I pray you will remember what I have taught you."

Yalda realized both her father and Uncle Croc were trying to keep her safe even though she sometimes did not like what they told her she could or could not do.

Parents, pause for a moment and ask your child(ren) these simple questions to encourage them to understand the truths presented so far.

Do you think that your parents are not as smart as you?

Do you listen to them when they give you advice?

How many times do your parents have to tell you to do something for you to listen to them and do it?

When your parents try to correct you for your mistakes, do you think they just want to bother you?

Do you know why your parents worry about you and try to help you make the right choices?

One day when Yalda went to Mr. Zhi's home to talk to him, he said, "My little girl, today I don't feel too good. I know you have questions, but please go to your father and ask him to help you. Tomorrow, come back and tell me what he tells you."

Yalda went to her father and talked to him about her situation. He talked to her very nicely and explained a lot of things he never had a chance to explain to her. She was so happy to see her father answer all her questions.

The next day, she went to see Mr. Zhi and asked him, "How do you feel today?"

He said, "I'm doing much better today. Did your father answer all your questions yesterday?"

She smiled and answered, "Yes, my dad made me so comfortable and answered all my questions. I came to visit you to tell you to thank you so much for everything you have been helping me with. Now, I see my dad can help me when I have a question, too."

Mr. Zhi was happy to hear her say that knowing her father was indeed a wise man and a great father.

Parents, pause for a moment and discuss how you and your child(ren) can better communicate when they have questions about life choices.

When you have a question about choices in your life, who do you turn to for advice?

Do you have anything you want help with?

Do you know you can trust me as your parent, and I will try my best to help you with it?

Little by little, Yalda became better in everything she did. She became one of the best-behaved and wisest children in the community. She listened, respected, and helped everyone in the community. When she had free time, she volunteered in any community that needed help.

She said, "When I grew up, I want to have the biggest daycare in my community. I want to share my knowledge with all kids around the world. I just want to explain to the world a little about life. Everyone wants to have a good life, and I want to help them understand what I have learned. The world needs to stand up and come together to share the truth of what they have learned. Love should be between us all the time."

"I especially want to help kids like Uncle Croc and my father helped me. I want kids to understand how important it is to listen to their parents. No one should be abused by anyone, but they need to be disciplined. Kids need to grow up learning what is right and what is wrong. They need to understand the consequences of their choices and not be disrespectful to their parents or teachers. All the kids need someone who cares for them, loves them, and teaches them how to grow love inside of them," she said.

"I would really like to see other communities work together like ours. The crocodiles and my hippo family all work together to make this a safe community to raise their children and have a good life. When leaders work together toward the same goal, everyone can benefit, especially the children. The leaders and the kids' parents should be on the same page when it comes to creating happy and safe communities. I want to get this message out to other communities, as well."

Uncle Croc was very pleased with Yalda's ideas and offered her more advice to consider, "I want you to help other children understand that their parents are there to love them and care for them. Parents and children should respect and appreciate each other. Please, my little girl, I know you are very smart. You have learned how to make good decisions, do things right, recover from your mistakes, stay away from trouble, always be true to yourself, and help others. My little girl, I want you to go out there and show the world the meaning of love and living the good life. Help them to understand what a family is for. My little girl, I have confidence in you. The world is waiting for you to share all that you have learned. Please be careful not to judge but share what you have learned with compassion. Remember to make decisions based on what is right not just on your feelings and emotions. When you love something, but you know it is not good for you, choose to do what you know is right. That way you will help yourself and others."

Yalda grew up to be a wise teacher and leader in her community. Other leaders would come to her for advice just like she did with Uncle Croc.

Conclusion

I have shared this story with parents, teachers, and students around the world. I understand we may do and think differently, however, we all should diligently seek the truth. Like tending a garden takes time to produce good results, our kids need our patience to grow into healthy productive adults. Remember all the kids don't learn the same way. Some of them are fast learners and some of them are slow learners. We just need to be patient with them and give them our love. Our kids are like trees. They need to grow roots to become healthy trees. We need to take great care of our children and help them to grow roots so they will grow up to be strong and healthy adults. This is how we can impact the next generation and change the world.

Notes For Parents

We need to seek to understand our kids better than we understand ourselves. When we were young, we probably did worse things than they have done. We need to forgive our kids more easily than ourselves. We know kids can say anything when they get mad, but that doesn't mean they mean it. I truly believe, if we are patient and tell them how to do things the right way, they will have a better chance to do better than we did. We need to start disciplining our kids when they are little like the wise crocodile did with the young hippo. The older they get the harder it will be to discipline them.

My fellow parents, our kids are dependent on us to teach them to do things right. Every family wants to have their child grow up to be the president, prime minister, governor, mayor, etc. We are supposed to love them, respect them, appreciate we have them, and show them the realities of life so they can become good leaders. You especially need to know who their friends are and be aware of their activities. Sometimes, their friends are the ones who get them into trouble. Don't forget this world is full of influences that can draw your child away from doing what is right and acting selfishly. Our lives should be examples of how to make healthy choices in life.

If you have already learned these lessons as a parent, you need to help other parents who are struggling with their kids. Go to Facebook, Instagram, Twitter, etc., and share your recipe for helping your kids with others. We all know no family is perfect. We all go through the same problems with our kids. The Lord will bless you and your kids when you do your part by taking care of and teaching your children what is right. Remember to set an example of doing what is right for your kids and for other parents.

Notes To Children

C hildren, you need to understand that our lives grow as we learn to trust one another. Yes, you need to be careful who you trust. Often, jealousy causes their minds to turn to evil. It can make them do a lot of unnecessary and hurtful things to others. They may be jealous of the life and family you have and say or do unpleasant things to you. The problem is some have let their love for others fade away little by little and become replaced by envy and hate.

However, you cannot let what one or two others have done or said out of jealousy make you not trust anybody. You cannot live in this world without learning who to trust and begin to build your relationships on trust. You will not be able to have a good life in this world without trusting one another.

Another area you need to understand is you need to learn to respect one another. It will be very difficult for you if you do not learn to respect your parents, teachers, and leaders. If you were to meet the President of the United States or the Queen of England, you would need to speak with them with respect. I want you to also understand that the biggest heroes in your lives should be your parents. Even though he or she makes mistakes, or you have misunderstandings, you need to treat them with respect. You need to remember how they have done things to make you happy and try to help you prepare to be productive adults. That should be special enough to earn your respect.

There are a few things we all need to stay away from: selfishness, wickedness, anger, and hate. Our feelings and emotions need to be focused on making our world a better place. Perhaps, we have not had a good relationship with our parents. Please remember we all have different types of problems, but we all need to handle our problems the right way and learn to control our emotions. If not, these problems cause division and fighting instead of peace and cooperation.

Listen, our lives are a blessing. We should thank the Lord and appreciate the fact we have life. I want you to understand that you know who you are and where you are right now, but you do not know where you will be and who you will turn out to be in your future. However, what you can be in the future doesn't have anything to do with good luck or bad luck. Yes, life can be full of surprises. How you handle these surprises will begin to create who you will be and what you will accomplish in your future.

You need to look at these surprises as opportunities to grow and learn and appreciate them. You should never blame anyone for things that happen in your life. Life is just like school. As long as you live, you will learn from it every day of your life. This is the reason why when something bad happens to you, you need to use that experience to learn from it. My parents always said, "It's better to learn from it today than let it interfere with your tomorrow." When someone does something bad to you, you should not respond in anger. Forgiving is the best way to keep anger from controlling your emotions. You need to delete anything from your mind that can stop you from moving forward. It doesn't matter who you are or where you come from. You can achieve success if you have a positive mindset and never let it fade away.

I know for sure your world will be better than ours, but please keep it real. You need to try your best to follow the rules and the laws of your country. A country without rules and laws is a place of chaos and destruction. If you let everyone come up with their own rules and laws in the country, it will eventually destroy itself and the good people will leave.

In our story, we read how working together and supporting each other are the best options to make everyone live a blessed life. I want you to understand that very well. The day the Lord introduced you to this world, you were born for a reason. Please try to understand that as long as you breathe, you are alive, but that doesn't mean that you have life.

The Lord created us to have life and enjoy our lives to the end of our time here on earth. Each of us enjoys life differently and do different things to make ourselves happy, but that doesn't mean we are so different we can't get along with one another. We are the same and we are connected in a special way because we are all God's children. God created the earth to provide for us and we all need to work together to take great care of it.

Life is almost like a game, but you need to know how to play it to come out successfully. You are part of a team that must work together so all of you get to your destination successfully. Before you and I were born, our parents walked on the dirt road to reach their destination. They chose to work together with those of their generation to make things better so now you and I have wonderful, paved roads with so many different ways to get to our destinations.

Now, it is your job to work with those of your generation to use the equipment and support you have been given to make your world a better place than our generation was able to accomplish. All you need to do is take what God has given you and use it to be the person this world needs you to become. Don't be deceived into taking the easy way to walk through life. It will turn out to be the hard way to becoming who you want and need to be to achieve your own personal success and become a world changer.

Helping Other Children

W e need to try to help other children to have a better life. We are taught to know the difference between right and wrong, but sometimes we make wrong or poor choices. Then we might be labeled as bad and placed in juvenile detention centers. If we do we do what is right, this does not have to happen to us. Let us be patient and help guide those other children who have made bad choices. We need to try to find the good part of them. We need to help them use their intelligence constructively. Those kids have a special love inside of them. We need to look for it to find it. Where they are right now should be a place to teach them how to grow love inside of them. We should ask them what they want to do in life, and we should help their dreams comes true. We already know sports help kids stay out of trouble. Let us introduce them to all the different types of sports. There are so many things we can do with our family to help other children and make them feel special and show them it doesn't matter who they are or where they come from.

My favorite actors used to be Sylvester Stallone, Jean Claude Van Damme, Arnold Schwarzenegger, and Jackie

Chan. Do you know why? These actors played characters who didn't let anything hold them back, nothing was too high to reach, and nothing was too hard to complete. We need to help each other to come out of our shells and not think someone is unteachable. If we are patient in helping them, anyone can get it right.

I came from a country of bullies. When I was growing up, I saw so many kids who were born into difficult situations. My country didn't offer any help to those kids. They were bullied by other kids, and they grew up to become bullies.

We all are perfect just the way we were created by the Lord. However, every talent the Lord has given to us should be used in a positive way. Some kids choose to use their talents the wrong way. If the kids are good at lying, stealing or anything we know is not right, we can try to put them in the same field that works with the things they are doing. For example, if they lie or steal, have them research the law, judges, and how undercover cops work with crime scenes. They need to do things right for the country, their family, and their life. Teach them when they steal because they don't have the money to buy something that there are ways they can earn the money and do it right. Remind them it takes a thief to know a thief and they can turn what they have learned into a career of catching thieves. We need to teach them how to turn bad into good, fighting into peace, and bad luck into a blessing. We need to work with them to get them to seek to do life the right way and that they will prosper when they do things God's way.

A Note To Parents

We know our kids are our shadows. They are a reflection of us. They are going to say and do things they see us do. Our actions speak louder than our words. We have the opportunity to influence our children and help them become healthy and productive adults. Let us be aware of our influence and realize we are very lucky to have them. We need to see the beauty and great potential in them. My parents used to tell me the reason the world is in a such mess is because we seem to appreciate things more than we do our children and what God has blessed us within our lives.

Having kids is a big responsibility. We need to take great care of our kids and teach them what is right. We need to do our part, teach them about the love of our heavenly Father, how to do things right, and how God will guide them. Then the blessings of God will flow into their lives.

Team Parents

We need to work together to create a system we will call Team Parents. I am putting together a website for everyone who wants to donate. All the money will go to the parents who really need help to raise their kids. We will make sure the money goes to parents around the world, so they have opportunities to live a better life. We all need to help others who are struggling and show them how they can really get themselves out of their misery. If they want someone to adopt their kids, if you can, we will connect you to them. We need to help them without taking their kids away from them so their families can remain together no matter what. Let us be the children of God who will hold each other's hands without thinking of our color, sex, race, or religion. We are all equal in the eyes of our heavenly Father.

We all were kids, and we know how we were when we were younger. We know for sure that our kids don't like to listen to us just like we didn't like to listen to our parents. That doesn't mean we should let them fail. We know kids should learn from our mistakes. They may say they won't do stupid things like their parents, but they might do things worse than we did. Sometimes, we can't keep them from getting hurt. We must warn them and then be willing to support them and remind them of their mistakes until they can get themselves on the right track.

Every single day, I learned about both good and bad by observing the behavior of our kids. We need to understand this is part of life. Our kids are our hearts and without having a healthy foundation for life, they will not learn to make safe and right choices for themselves. It's like a tree without healthy roots can never be a healthy tree. Learning from your kids today can be the best movie entertainment you will ever want to see. I just want to remind you, even though all of us want our kids to be like us, we need to remember we didn't want to be like our parents. If you are doing a good job teaching them how to make good life choices, you just need to keep up with it knowing it will plant good seed within them. The Bible says if we train them in the way they should go, when they are older they will not choose the wrong path (Proverbs 22:6).

We need to be cautious about wanting or not wanting others to help train our children. We should seek advice from those who not only possess good knowledge or education about parenting, but that have shown they use these things to teach their children the right ways to handle life situations. Our kids do need a good education to navigate through life. We need to use ourselves as an example. We should work together and take each other's knowledge and wrap it in a gift wrap and give it to our kids.

We say we want to protect our kids, but we need to make sure they don't fall into the same hole and make the same mistakes we did. Especially if it was a dark hole. We all went into a hole at some point in our lives. Some holes were deeper or darker than others. Let us teach our kids the truth about life so they won't have to go through what we want through. As loving parents who want the best for our kids, let us teach our kids to choose the right way in this world even though we missed it.

It doesn't matter their race, religion, color, or sex. They all should be treated the same and have the right to be who they were designed by God to be.

These are some questions I would like you to answer.

Do you love and take great care of your kids?

Do you think that you should do things a parent should do for their kids?

Do your kids respect and appreciate you as a parent?

If not, did you show them how by respecting them and others?

Will you give your life to save your kids' life?

Please, say a few special things about your kids to your kids.

Do they know they are special and have a destiny and a purpose?

Do you believe your kids are the best-behaved kids in the world?

If yes or no, why?

When it comes to bad behavior, do you believe that your kids are the worst ones?

If yes, why?

Do your kids sometimes listen to you and sometimes not?

If yes, what do you do to make them listen?

Do you take time to know your kids?

Do you believe our kids are watching everything we do and will use some of it to blame us for the things they do?

Do you believe other parents are not going through the same thing you are going through?

Do you believe our kids always need our love and support even though they say they don't?

Are you the head and tail of your family?

How do you feel as a single parent?

Do you believe a woman needs a man or a man needs a woman to take great care of their kids?

> *If yes, why?*

Do you trust and believe in your kids?

> *If not, why?*

Do you believe good kids will always be good and bad kids will always be bad?

> *If yes, why?*

Do you give your kids a chance to fix their mistakes or show them how to repair their mistakes?

Do you know, even though we can't delete mistakes, we can repair the damage and learn from them?

What do you do when you get caught doing something wrong?

Do you believe in forgiveness?

What makes you a good parent?

Do you believe, that as long as you have kids, you are automatically a good parent?

Are you a good example for your kids?

Do you take your kids to church?

Do you explain to them why?

Do you explain to your kids about good and bad, right or wrong?

   If yes, do you ever give them opportunities to use what you are teaching them?

Don't you believe, when a child reaches the age of fifteen they should know how to handle an emergency situation?

Do you believe a child should be alone as long as he or she has turned eighteen?

Do you believe our kids shouldn't need our help after they turn eighteen?

Is there any time a parent shouldn't be part of their kids' life?

Don't you believe our family love should be forever?

What is the difference between a rich family and a poor family?

What is the meaning of family?

Do you think that your first help in raising your children should come from your family when you need it?

Do you believe we are a big family who should help each other with all our problems?

If not, why?

We say we shouldn't judge a book by its cover, so why do we judge each other based on color, culture, or religion?

They said actions speak louder than words, is that true?

Do you believe we should love all our kids the same, even though some of them are different?

I want you to understand, that I'm not telling you how to raise your kids. I just want to share my knowledge with you.